The Guest Who Forgot to Leave

by Mira Antares
illustrated by Anna Rich

Harcourt

Orlando   Boston   Dallas   Chicago   San Diego

Visit *The Learning Site!*

www.harcourtschool.com

The sun was just coming up. It was very quiet in the house. Susan Baldwin's parents were still sleeping, but Susan was awake. She had gotten up very early and had gotten dressed. It was Saturday. That meant no school today. Susan's friend Keisha had invited her to join her family for a picnic in the park.

Susan tiptoed through the living room and through the hall to the front door. She opened the door to check the weather. A cool breeze greeted her. She could smell the grass and trees in her front yard. It was a beautiful day.

She glanced up and down the street. There was
no traffic. It was too early. Suddenly Susan heard a
crying sound. "What was that?" she wondered. The
sound had come from right in front of the door.
Susan looked down. There, by her feet, was a little
ball of gray fur! It was a little kitten, all curled up.

Susan knelt down next to the kitten. The kitten raised its head, took one look at her, and began to meow. Susan asked the little creature, "What are you doing here, kitty? Where did you come from? How did you get here?" The kitten kept crying, and Susan wanted to help it. "Are you hungry?" she asked.

Susan went inside to the kitchen. She found a
can of tuna and put some of it in a little bowl. She
went back outside and put the bowl on the ground.
The little kitten began to eat at once. "I'm glad you
like that tuna!" said Susan.

At breakfast, Susan told her parents about the
kitten. They all wondered how the little kitten
found its way to their front door.

Later, when Susan got home from the picnic, the
kitten was still sitting by her front door. It ran to
Susan and cried. Susan's parents said she could feed
it one more time.

The next day, Susan looked to see if the kitten was still there. The kitten had never left the front door. Susan brought food out to the kitten that day, and the next.

On the third day, the weather turned cold. A heavy rain was falling. When Susan opened the front door in the morning, she found the kitten huddled into a ball. It was soaking wet and crying. Susan asked her parents if she could bring the kitten inside. "It will only be for a short visit," said Susan. "The kitten will be our guest. I promise it won't impose on you."

"It's all right if it stays here for only a couple of days," said Mr. Baldwin. "Maybe its owner will show up, or maybe we can find a home for it."

Susan ran to get the kitten and brought it inside. "What shall I call you?" she asked the kitten. The kitten was happy to be inside. It ran around and climbed all over Susan. "I guess I'll call you Frisky," said Susan.

The days went by quickly. Susan was growing
more attached to Frisky with each passing day. The
kitten began to act as if the house belonged to him.
He rubbed against the walls and the furniture. This
was Frisky's way of marking his territory.

One of Mr. Baldwin's pastimes was to sit in his favorite chair and watch the evening news on TV. This was how he relaxed when he came home from work. One day, he was just about to sit down when he noticed Frisky sitting in his chair! "What are you doing in my chair? If you're trying to annoy me, you're doing a good job of it," he said irritably.

Susan came into the room just then and heard him. "Dad, Frisky doesn't mean to get in the way. I'm sure he doesn't want to impose on you."

"I thought he was going to be our guest for just a few days," Mr. Baldwin said glumly. "What happened? Did you forget to leave?" he asked Frisky irritably.

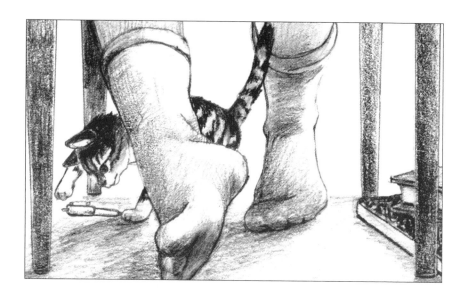

Susan picked Frisky up and took him into her room. He played around her feet while she did her homework. Susan would have asked her father to tutor her in her new science lesson, but she and Frisky had upset him. Every so often, she stopped working in order to pet Frisky. Susan was beginning to fear that her parents would make her give Frisky away.

The next afternoon, Mrs. Baldwin sat down at the kitchen table to read the newspaper. This was one of her favorite pastimes. There was plenty of room to spread out the paper. She was about to begin reading when the Baldwins' furry guest leaped up on the table. Of course, Frisky decided to sit down right in the middle of the newspaper. There he sat, purring.

"Susan, come here now!" called Mrs. Baldwin. Susan came running from her room. "Our guest has worn out his welcome," Mrs. Baldwin said glumly. "I think it's time for him to move on."

"But, Mom," said Susan, "Frisky doesn't mean to impose on us. He just wants attention. Please don't make me give him away! Please, Mom!"

Just then, Mr. Baldwin came home. He looked at his wife and daughter and asked, "What's going on here? I hope you haven't begun to bicker over that cat."

Susan said, "No, Dad, we would never bicker over the cat. We are just having a talk about Frisky. He doesn't mean to cause trouble. Look at the way he's sitting on that newspaper. You can see how happy he is. Can you hear him purring? He has a fine disposition. I hope you're not carrying a grudge against him because he sat in your chair yesterday."

"Susan," said Mrs. Baldwin, "if Frisky keeps sitting on my newspaper, he is going to ruin my disposition. I will be the one carrying a grudge!"

"I have an idea," said Mr. Baldwin. "Frisky is a very young cat. The reason he is causing trouble around here is that he's never been trained. Susan, would you be willing to train him?"

"Of course, Dad, if you'll help me," Susan answered eagerly.

"I can tutor you about training cats, and if Frisky can learn to behave, he can be a member of the Baldwin family. That is, if your mother agrees," Dad explained.

Mrs. Baldwin looked at her husband and then at Susan. She seemed to be thinking very hard. Then she smiled. "Actually, I think it's a great idea for Susan to train Frisky. How about starting by teaching him not to sit on my newspaper?"

"Oh, thank you! I love you both!" cried Susan. "I promise I'll train him. You'll see. Frisky will be the best behaved cat in the world! No one will have a reason to hold a grudge against him!"

As they talked, Frisky continued to sit in the middle of Mrs. Baldwin's newspaper. He obviously enjoyed being in the middle of things. He hadn't stopped purring for one moment. If the Baldwins had looked closely at him, they would have noticed that Frisky was smiling!